TED SAW AN EGG

By Judy Kentor Schmauss
Illustrated by Len Epstein

Table of Contents

Illustrations on pages 21–23 created by Carol Stutz

All inquiries should be addressed to:
Barron's Educational Series, Inc.
250 Wireless Boulevard
Hauppauge, New York 11788
www.barronseduc.com

Library of Congress Catalog Card No.: 2005054871

ISBN-13: 978-0-7641-3283-4
ISBN-10: 0-7641-3283-0

Library of Congress Cataloging-in-Publication Data
Schmauss, Judy Kentor.
Ted saw an egg / Judy Kentor Schmauss.
p. cm. – (Reader's clubhouse)
Summary: Ted finds a very large egg, from which an equally large chick hatches. Includes facts about eggs, a related activity, and word list.
ISBN-13: 978-0-7641-3283-4
ISBN-10: 0-7641-3283-0
(1. Eggs—Fiction. 2. Chickens—Fiction. 3. Animals—Infancy—Fiction) I. Title. II. Series.

PZ7.S34736Ted2006
(E)—dc22

2005054871

PRINTED IN CHINA
9 8 7 6 5 4 3 2 1

Dear Parent and Educator,

Welcome to the Barron's Reader's Clubhouse, a series of books that provide a phonics approach to reading.

Phonics is the relationship between letters and sounds. It is a system that teaches children that letters have specific sounds. Level 1 books introduce the short-vowel sounds. Level 2 books progress to the long-vowel sounds. This progression matches how phonics is taught in many classrooms.

Ted Saw an Egg introduces the short "e" sound. Simple words with this short-vowel sound are called **decodable words.** The child knows how to sound out these words because he or she has learned the sound they include. This story also contains **high-frequency words.** These are common, everyday words that the child learns to read by sight. High-frequency words help ensure fluency and comprehension. **Challenging words** go a little beyond the reading level. The child will identify these words with help from the illustration on the page. All words are listed by their category on page 24.

Here are some coaching and prompting statements you can use to help a young reader read *Ted Saw an Egg:*

- **On page 4, "Ted" is a decodable word. Point to the word and say:**

  Read this word. How did you know the word? What sounds did it make?

  Note: There are many opportunities to repeat the above instruction throughout the book.

- **On page 17, "shell" is a challenging word. Point to the word and say:**

  Read this word. What is the outside of the egg called? It rhymes with "well." How did you know the word? Did you look at the picture? How did it help?

You'll find more coaching ideas on the Reader's Clubhouse Web site: *www.barronsclubhouse.com.* Reader's Clubhouse is designed to teach and reinforce reading skills in a fun way. We hope you enjoy helping children discover their love of reading!

Sincerely,

Nancy Harris

Nancy Harris
Reading Consultant

Ted saw an egg.

He saw a red egg.

Ted bent down.

He saw a BIG, red egg.

Ted saw a speck on the egg.

It is not a speck, said Ted.

Ted saw a leg.

Ted saw a leg come out.

Ted saw two legs.

Two legs came out.

Ted let out a yell.

Look at my egg.

Now there is no egg.

Now there is a shell.

I have a new pet, said Ted.

It is my best pet yet!

Fun Facts About

Eggs

- Many animals lay eggs. Fish lay lots of eggs. The ocean sunfish produces 30 million eggs at one time.

- The largest dinosaur egg ever found measured 12 inches (30 centimeters). That's about as long as an adult human's foot!

- A chicken normally lays between 1 and 5 eggs at a time.

• It takes about 3 weeks from the time an egg is laid until a baby chick hatches:

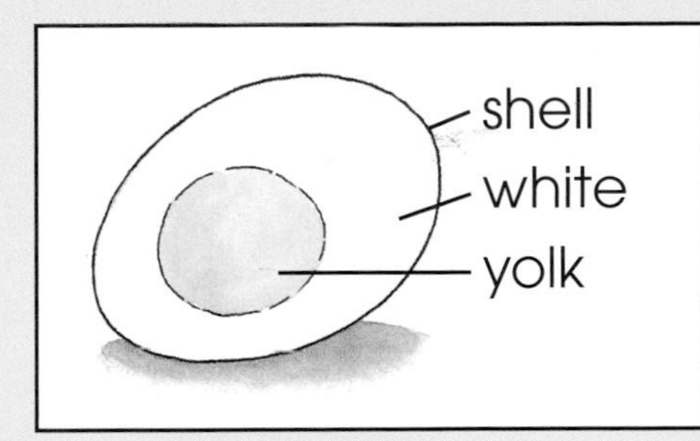

A new egg

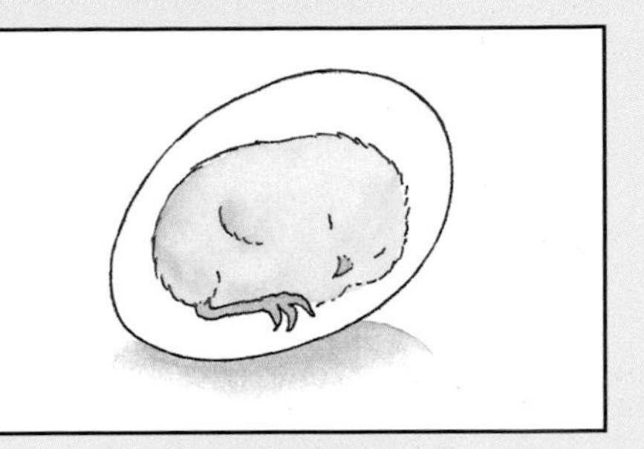

The egg after 1 week

The chick begins to hatch after 3 weeks

A fully hatched chick

Rabbit Eggs

You will need:

- plastic egg that can be opened into halves (such as a plastic Easter egg)
- 2 large white pompoms
- small pink pompom
- 2 sheets of construction paper (white and pink)
- 2 pipe cleaners
- glue
- safety scissors
- 2 googly eyes (the bigger the better)
- small toy or candy

1. With the construction paper, cut two large white rabbit ears. Cut two smaller pink ovals. Glue the pink pieces inside the white pieces.

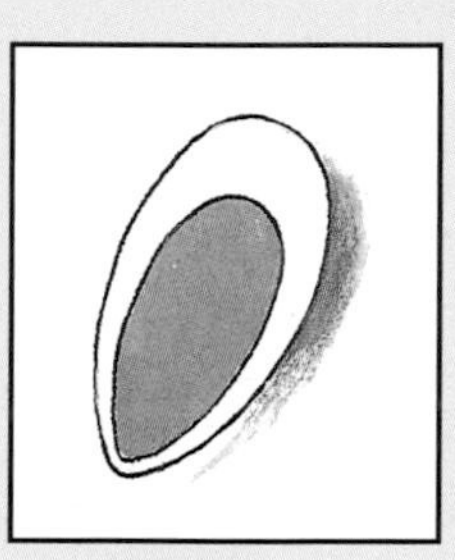

2. Glue the ears to the top of the pointy end of the egg, leaving some space between them.

3. Glue the two white pompoms on the front of the egg just above where the egg opens up. These will be the rabbit's cheeks.

4. Glue the pink pompom in the top center of the white pompoms for the rabbit's nose.

5. Cut the pipe cleaners into six pieces. Glue the pieces under each pompom for the rabbit's whiskers.

6. Glue on the eyes. Put candy, stickers, or a small toy inside your bunny for a special treat or a gift.

Word List

Challenging Words	shell	
Short E Decodable Words	bent best egg leg legs let pet speck Ted	yell yet
High-Frequency Words	a an at big came come down have he I is it look	my new no not now on out red said saw the there two